Adapted by Nancy E. Krulik
Based on the motion picture written by Jonathan Betuel

THEODORE REX

SCHOLASTIC INC.

New York   Toronto   London   Auckland   Sydney

ISBN 0-590-67785-3

Photo Credits
All interior photos Suzanne Hanover
Cover and title page photos of Theodore Rex by Blake Little
Cover photo of Whoopi Goldberg by Suzanne Hanover

12 11 10 9 8 7 6 5 4 3 2 1   5 6 7 8 9/9 0/0

Printed in the U.S.A.   14

First Scholastic Printing, December 1995

CHAPTER ONE

The eight-foot-tall, three-thousand-pound dinosaur got out of his car, straightened his tie, and wandered over to the crime scene. No one even gave him a second look. Dinosaurs are no big deal in the twenty-first century. In the twenty-first century, dinosaurs and humans live side by side, working together with mutual respect.

"What's it to you, scale?" a rookie police officer snarled as the dinosaur looked over his shoulder.

Okay, maybe they don't have a *lot* of mutual respect. But dinosaurs do live in the same Grid as humans. They dress like humans, and hold jobs like humans. And now it seemed dinosaurs had something else in common with humans—they were being murdered.

The giant dinosaur pulled out his police-department badge and showed it to one of the officers. "Rex, Teddy Rex," he said. "Grid Police Department Public Relations." Teddy turned to the rookie who had insulted him. "We're not scales," he said, shaking his tail. "We're dinos. How would you like it if I called you 'softskin'?"

Teddy looked over the rookie's head and spotted Sarah Jiminez, a veteran human police detective, examining the body. Teddy walked straight over to her.

"It's awful, Sarah," Teddy said as he looked down at the dead dinosaur.

"He a Grid mate of yours?" Sarah asked.

"Well, yes . . . and no," Teddy answered. "I was home asleep, when all of a sudden I had a flash of something wrong."

Sarah nodded. That was nothing unusual. Everyone in the Grid knew that dinosaurs had some sort of dino sixth sense. They always seemed to be able to tell when one of their own was in trouble.

"But a dinocide," Teddy continued in amazement. "That's never happened before. Extinction, yes, but . . ." Teddy stopped in mid-sentence and sighed. "Do you have any clues?" he asked in his best police manner. Teddy may have worked only in the department's public relations office, but he still considered himself a cop.

Sarah shook her head. "No suspects, no evidence, no leads."

Teddy pulled out his portable holographic phone and called police headquarters. A hologram of a police officer appeared before Teddy's eyes. "Headquarters, where is Commissioner Lynch?" Teddy asked the ghostlike image. "It's an emergency."

"He's at a New Eden fund-raiser at the Explorer's Club," the hologram replied.

"I'm on my way!" Teddy said, and hung up his phone.

CHAPTER TWO

The New Eden Foundation was a group of scientists, scholars, and volunteers who worked together to save many species from becoming extinct. This evening they were having a fancy fund-raiser. Everyone was dressed in tuxedos and evening gowns. When Teddy barged in on the party, he really stood out because he was wearing his usual three-toed sneakers, slacks, and baseball cap. He was also the only dinosaur in the room.

Deputy Police Commissioner Alex Summers was the first to spot him. "Teddy, I didn't know you were a million-credit-chip donor to the New Eden Foundation," he said sarcastically. Summers hated dinosaurs of any species.

"I'm not," Teddy answered him. "I'm looking for Commissioner Lynch." Teddy looked over Deputy Commissioner Summers's head. "Ah-ha, there he is now." And before Summers could stop him, Teddy waddled his way right into the ballroom.

Commissioner Lynch was very surprised to see Teddy. But he introduced him to the people he was speaking with, anyway. "Elizar Kane, may I introduce Teddy Rex, Assistant Press Officer with the Grid Police Department."

But Teddy and Mr. Kane had already met. Mr. Kane was the founder of the New Eden Foundation. He was also the scientist who had re-created the dinosaurs and brought them to life in the twenty-first century.

"Teddy is my crowning achievement," Mr. Kane said proudly. "He must be an asset to the police department."

Teddy and Commissioner Lynch walked over to an empty corner to speak in private. "There's been a murder in the carnival graveyard, sir," Teddy said. "A dinocide."

The police commissioner was shocked. He motioned across the room to Deputy Commissioner Summers. Summers made his way over to the commissioner.

"Sir, is there something wrong?"

"There's been a dinocide," the commissioner answered him.

Teddy couldn't hold back any longer. He looked straight down at the top of Commissioner Lynch's head and spoke. "Beg pardon, sir, but I'd like to be assigned to the case. As a detective."

The two men stared at him. Teddy worked in the public relations department! He didn't even carry a gun.

"I joined the force to be a detective," Teddy explained. "I was trained to walk the streets, not give Grid tours. And we *are* talking about a dinocide here."

Deputy Commissioner Summers was getting nervous. This dinocide could mean a lot of trouble. He pulled the commissioner away and whispered in his ear.

"Boss, this case is a hot one," he said. "When news of this gets out, there could be riots—dinosaurs on the rampage and humans striking back."

Now the commissioner was nervous, too. "A big-time crime like this could kill my law-and-order campaign when I run for mayor," he said with a shudder.

The two men looked back over at Teddy. He was busy sneaking cookies from a tray.

"What about our tall and shiny prince over there?" Summers asked. "We could make him our first dino detective."

The commissioner looked confused.

"Track this one with me, sir," Summers explained. "Teddy solves the dinocide. Who's the hero?"

"Teddy Rex?" guessed the commissioner.

Summers shook his head. "No — Lynch: the commissioner who had the vision to look beyond species to save the town. Forget about being mayor. Think senator."

Senator! That was all the commissioner needed to hear. The case was Teddy's. But just to be sure, the commissioner was pairing him with an experienced cop.

"We're teaming you up for your own good," Commissioner Lynch told Teddy.

"With a veteran, a pro," Summers added with a nasty smile. He knew just the right police officer for Teddy. That pain-in-the-neck cop, Katie Coltrane.

CHAPTER THREE

Katie Coltrane was just back on active duty after a leave of absence. And her attitude was . . . well . . . not the best. While other officers defined their job with three magic words, *preserve, protect,* and *commission,* Katie had her own three magic words. **This job stinks.**

Katie was just coming home from work when her beeper sounded. The commissioner was ordering her to a New Eden fund-raiser. So much for getting a little shut-eye.

When Katie arrived at the Explorer's Club, Commissioner Lynch, Deputy Commissioner Summers, and Teddy were waiting outside.

"There's been a homicide," Summers told her with an evil grin, "and your name came up."

"Actually, it's a dinocide," Teddy corrected him.

"Like extinct?" Katie asked.

"Like murdered," Teddy explained.

The commissioner stood beside Teddy. "Teddy Rex, meet Katie Coltrane," he said, introducing them. "You two solve this case together. Teddy's in Public Relations, but I'm promoting him to the field, temporarily."

This isn't happening, Katie thought. She looked from the commissioner, to Summers, to Teddy. Oh gosh. It really was happening. "Suppose something goes wrong," she said in a panic. "I'm no dino-sitter."

Summers was getting annoyed. "Teddy graduated from the academy just like you did," he said.

"So what am I? An extension course? I'll be the laughingstock of the department!" Katie shouted at him.

Commissioner Lynch stood tall and glared at Katie. "Get me results by prime time tomorrow," he ordered. "The official log will show this is *not* a request."

Katie and Teddy watched as the two men left and went back to the party.

"Just what do you do in Public Relations?" Katie asked Teddy.

"I give tours to visiting dignitaries," the dinosaur answered proudly.

"I'm working with a tour guide?!" Katie looked at him in disbelief.

CHAPTER FOUR

It was almost dawn when the fund-raiser at the Explorer's Club ended. Deputy Commissioner Summers took a ride home in Mr. Kane's limo. Limousines had been outlawed years ago because they used too much fuel. But it seemed Mr. Kane wasn't as dedicated to saving the Earth as people thought. Then again, Deputy Police Commissioner Summers wasn't as dedicated to police work as people thought, either.

"This dinocide thing could blow up in our faces," Summers said to Mr. Kane. "But I think I took care of it. I made the commissioner assign the Rex murder to the department's token dino. The scale begged Lynch to be a real detective. It's his dream or something. Then I teamed the little scale up with Coltrane from Gun Command. She's just back from leave."

Mr. Kane laughed. "The blind leading the blind."

Summers nodded. "Those two will never trace the murder back to you. They fail, we succeed." Summers motioned to the limo driver. "This is where I get out."

As Summers got out of the limo, Mr. Kane leaned forward to talk to his associate, Edge, who was sitting in the front seat.

"A scale detective is a sideshow," Edge said with a laugh.

But Kane wasn't so sure. He had created Teddy to be intelligent, honest, and loyal. That could be dangerous—especially when paired with a trained policewoman.

"Have them followed," Mr. Kane ordered Edge. "I don't want anyone to sense our concern. And you know how I feel about failure, Edge. It reeks of imperfection. Any setback, and I will hold you personally responsible."

14

CHAPTER FIVE

It wasn't going to be hard for Edge and his band of Zapheads to keep an eye on Katie and Teddy. Those two would be hard to miss. There weren't too many dinosaur/human couples driving around in a dino-sized Rex Cruiser.

As the two drove around the city streets, Katie tried to duck down below the window.

"What's wrong?" Teddy asked.

"I don't want anyone from the department to see me in this," she answered him. Then she changed the subject. "I'm scared to ask, but what's next?"

"Well, let's see." Teddy thought out loud. "This is a dinocide."

Katie rolled her eyes. "Very good," she said sarcastically.

Teddy ignored her. "In a case like this, the detective first determines the cause of death," he recited, remembering the directions in his police handbook.

Katie nodded. "Right. But there's never been a dinocide before. Where would they do a dino autopsy?"

Teddy thought for a moment. "I got it!" he cried out.

Screeech! Teddy floored the gas pedal and sped off to the Museum of Natural History. After all, they'd been keeping dead dinos there for centuries!

The museum was dark and quiet. So quiet, in fact, that Teddy and Katie had to wake the night guard. She opened her eyes, took one look at Teddy, and screamed.

"Sorry, ma'am," Teddy said politely. He showed her his badge. "Could you please tell us where they brought the deceased?"

The night guard didn't have a clue as to what Teddy was talking about. "The deceased?" she asked.

Katie was losing patience. "The dead dino," she explained. "Does that ring a bell?"

The guard nodded. "Through the hall of reptiles and follow the stench to the dinosaurology lab."

Teddy sighed as they walked through the hall of reptiles. Dinosaur skeletons from centuries past lined the walls. "Museums give me the blues," he explained. "It's like I feel my ancestors looking down at me from across time. They want me to always do the best I can. Give one hundred percent."

Katie wasn't one for this kind of sentimental slobber. "Please," she snorted.

Teddy looked at her knowingly. "I just keep hoping your species will wake up before you become extinct like everything else around here."

"I keep hoping I'll wake up from this case. . . ." Katie muttered under her breath.

Finally they reached the dinosaurology lab. A small woman in a white lab coat joined them. She was Dr. Lila Amitraj, head dinosaurologist at the museum.

"We're investigating this dinocide," Teddy explained.

Dr. Amitraj looked surprised. She'd never seen a dino detective before. Of course, up until now, nobody else had, either.

Teddy started his investigation. He took a small light and shined it on the dino's snout. Then he removed something from the wound. It looked like a small metal wing.

17

"Dr. Amitraj, send this to the lab," he said, handing her the evidence. "Maybe they can reconstruct whatever it was." Teddy looked back at the body. "And now, prints. We dinos don't have fingerprints," he explained to Katie. "But the scale patterns on our tails are all different."

Teddy took the dino's tail, dipped it in ink, and pressed it on a piece of paper. Then he ran the print through a nearby computer. Almost immediately, the computer identified the victim.

"Oliver Rex, unemployed, resides at 35 Prehistoric Place with a Molly Rex."

Teddy gasped. Molly Rex was probably the most famous dino singer in the whole Grid. She performed every night at the Extinct Species Club.

CHAPTER SIX

As soon as Katie walked into the Extinct Species Club, she knew it was going to be a long night. First, she was greeted with an odd odor. "Ewww! What's that smell?" she asked.

"Clean air," Teddy answered. Dinos had a great love for things like clean air and clear water—things humans had neglected decades ago.

Katie and Teddy took their seats. There was a loud drumroll as Molly Rex took the stage. Teddy's eyes bulged. She was the most beautiful dino he'd ever seen.

"That girl-o-saurus is trouble," Katie warned. But Teddy wasn't listening. As soon as Molly finished singing, he grabbed some flowers from the table and followed her to her dressing room.

"Have we met?" Molly asked as Teddy presented her with the floral arrangement. She took a quick sniff of the flowers, then ate the whole bouquet in one dainty chomp.

"My partner and I saw your act," Teddy began.

"Partner?" Molly interrupted.

"Grid Police," Katie informed her. "And we're not here for your autograph."

Molly looked at Katie and shook her head. "You'd catch more bees with honey," she said sweetly.

Katie frowned. "We're after a killer, not bees, *honey*. The murderer of Oliver Rex."

Molly was stunned. Oliver was her friend; her roommate. And now he was dead. Whatever Molly could do to help them find his killer, she would. She started by telling Teddy and Katie everything she knew about Oliver.

"Oliver was a New Eden volunteer. He said it was Earth's only hope," Molly explained.

Teddy handed Molly his business card. "If you think of anything else, here's my number. And please, call me Teddy."

Molly shook her head. "I'll call you Theo. And my close friends call me Molly."

"Mine just call me collect," Katie added gruffly.

Teddy was still grinning as he and Katie left the club. Katie gave him a dirty look. This was one lovesick lizard. And Katie knew lovesick lizards didn't make great cops. They made *mistakes*. Katie was going to have to keep a special eye on Teddy.

CHAPTER SEVEN

The next morning, Katie was in a fighting mood. She was tired and hungry, and sitting in Teddy's uncomfortable car had left her achy. As soon as she and Teddy entered police headquarters, she walked up to the desk sergeant and looked him in the eye. "It's like this, Sarge," she barked. "My back aches, and I haven't slept all night or seen real food. Now how about a Rex-friendly cruiser?"

"Read my badge," the sergeant barked back. "It says police, not mommy!"

"Look into my eyes," Katie said, grabbing him by the neck. "I'm out of patience."

The sergeant backed down. "You're in luck," he said sweetly. "I have the perfect vehicle."

Katie smiled smugly. She'd won that battle. At least, she thought she had. Then she discovered that the sarge's "perfect"

vehicle was a police-department garbage truck! If Katie hadn't been the laughingstock of the department before, she was now!

To make matters worse, Police Commissioner Lynch wasn't too happy with Teddy and Katie's performance. He called them into his office to yell at them. "A Gun and a dinosaur detective," he moaned. "This was Summers's idea." Suddenly the commissioner brightened. "I know, I'll blame him. That's what employees are for."

He turned back to Katie and Teddy. "Remember, this case had better be gift-wrapped by prime time tonight, or else!" The commissioner turned and left the room.

Katie looked over at Teddy. His uniform was a mess. She sighed. If Katie was going to be hanging around with a dino, at least he could be a *well-dressed* dino.

"Come with me," she told him.

CHAPTER EIGHT

Katie led Teddy over to the Grid Police supply offices and introduced him to her friend, the *very* fashionable Ella.

"Teddy, say hello to Ella," Katie introduced them. "Teddy's here to be a chic scale," she explained.

"I get the drift," Ella said. "An undercover dinosaur."

Katie smiled. "Make him blend."

Ella shook her head in disbelief. Make a dinosaur blend? Impossible. "Try the zoo," she muttered.

It took some time, but eventually Teddy found just the right set of clothes—jeans, hooded sweatshirt, leather jacket, and high-top sneakers. "I look like a real cop," he said proudly, looking at his reflection.

Katie watched with amusement as Teddy strutted to their police vehicle. "Where to?" Katie asked him.

"New Eden," Teddy responded matter-of-factly.

Katie almost flew out of her seat. "New Eden?!"

"Molly said Oliver was a New Eden volunteer," Teddy explained. He looked over at Katie's shocked expression. "You don't want to go there, do you?" he asked her.

Katie shook her head. "I'll go anywhere to solve a case," she began, "but Teddy, Elizar Kane eats billionaires for breakfast. And now you want to tie the richest man in the Grid to murder?!"

Teddy smiled. That was *exactly* what he had in mind. "Don't stress. Mr. Kane's a close personal friend."

Katie knew she had no choice. She agreed to go—but only after she stopped off to see a close personal friend of her own.

CHAPTER NINE

Katie wasn't close to many people. In fact, she wasn't close to anyone, except a ten-year-old boy named Sebastian. Sebastian was a real Grid Kid: tough, hanging out on the streets, playing war wheel hockey. Katie liked to check up on Sebastian once in a while, just to make sure he was okay.

Sebastian was a *little* surprised to see Katie teamed up with a dinosaur. But after all, he *was* a Grid Kid — he'd seen it all. Nothing shocked him. Sebastian simply handed Katie a hockey stick and went over to the net.

"Shoot on me!" he called to her.

Katie grinned. One by one she shot six balls at the net. Three scored. She passed the stick to Teddy. "You're on line," she challenged him.

Teddy handed the stick to a nearby kid. Then he grabbed his tail and . . . *Whap! Whap! Whap! Whap! Whap! Whap!* All six balls went zooming into the net! Sebastian and his pals were very impressed. Katie was, too, even though she wouldn't admit it.

Katie smiled happily as she and Teddy drove off. She just liked knowing the kid was all right. Katie might not have been so happy if she had known that Edge's Zapheads had been watching her and Sebastian, and that they'd videotaped the whole game. That couldn't be good.

CHAPTER TEN

Katie and Teddy looked around in amazement as they drove up to the gates of New Eden. It was the first time either of them had seen real live animals. Zebras, elephants, lions, giraffes, and rhinoceroses roamed the lawns.

"Amazing," Teddy said. "He has his own game park."

"The only place left in the Grid with real animals," Katie added.

"It's never open to the public," Teddy noted sadly.

But Teddy and Katie were *not* the public. They were police officers investigating a dinocide. And, at least for now, Mr. Kane was willing to cooperate with the investigation.

"Hello again, Theodore," Mr. Kane said graciously as Teddy and Katie entered his office. Mr. Kane reached out to shake Katie's hand. "Do you have a second?" he asked. "I've got something wonderful to show you."

Mr. Kane walked over to the lab table. There he had a large fish tank with frozen Ice Fish inside. Mr. Kane started to explain how Ice Fish could be frozen in ice for years and then brought back to life. Teddy seemed fascinated. Katie, however, was less than thrilled with how the conversation was going.

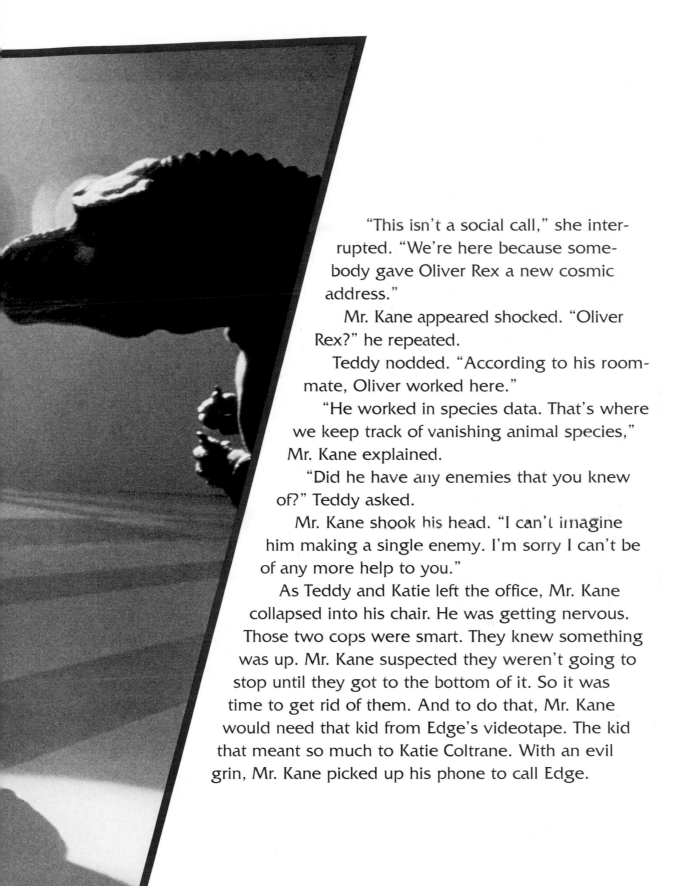

"This isn't a social call," she interrupted. "We're here because somebody gave Oliver Rex a new cosmic address."

Mr. Kane appeared shocked. "Oliver Rex?" he repeated.

Teddy nodded. "According to his roommate, Oliver worked here."

"He worked in species data. That's where we keep track of vanishing animal species," Mr. Kane explained.

"Did he have any enemies that you knew of?" Teddy asked.

Mr. Kane shook his head. "I can't imagine him making a single enemy. I'm sorry I can't be of any more help to you."

As Teddy and Katie left the office, Mr. Kane collapsed into his chair. He was getting nervous. Those two cops were smart. They knew something was up. Mr. Kane suspected they weren't going to stop until they got to the bottom of it. So it was time to get rid of them. And to do that, Mr. Kane would need that kid from Edge's videotape. The kid that meant so much to Katie Coltrane. With an evil grin, Mr. Kane picked up his phone to call Edge.

29

CHAPTER ELEVEN

Mr. Kane was right about one thing. Katie and Teddy weren't going to stop until they got to the bottom of the murders. Their next stop, in fact, was the funeral for Oliver Rex. Katie figured they might get some information from some of the mourning dinos. Teddy figured he might get a chance to walk Molly Rex home.

Teddy was the one who was right.

But Katie didn't like it. "That dinette is the Rex your mother warned you about," she whispered to Teddy.

"I don't have a mother. I'm a test-tube baby," Teddy reminded her. "Come on, Katie, look at it as a police escort."

There was nothing more Katie could do. She rolled her eyes as she watched Molly and Teddy wander off into their Prehistoric Place neighborhood.

* * *

Teddy was very nervous about being alone with Molly. But he thought he might just know the way to her heart. "I baked a few macadamia-chip cookies the other day," he told her, "from scratch."

Molly grinned. "How could I say no to a Rex who bakes cookies from scratch?" she said, batting her eyes. Together, the two happy dinos went up to Teddy's apartment for some cookies and tango music.

Molly and Teddy danced all evening long. "You're a wonderful dancer," Teddy complimented her. Molly smiled shyly and took his tail in hers.

Beep! Beep! Beep! The Rex romance was interrupted by the sound of Teddy's police beeper. He and Katie were being paged to police headquarters.

"I'll be back soon," he called to Molly as he walked out the door. "You can finish my cookies."

CHAPTER TWELVE

Teddy and Katie had been paged by Captain Alaric. He had some interesting information for them. It seemed that Oliver Rex had been killed by a . . . butterfly! Well, not a real butterfly. Real butterflies are extinct in the twenty-first century. This was a *mechanical* butterfly created by the world-famous horrible weapons maker, the Toymaker. The Toymaker had installed a bomb in the body of the little metal insect. The bomb had exploded on contact with Oliver Rex's snout.

It was time for Katie and Teddy to make a little visit to the Toymaker's workshop. But this toy workshop was not the kind of place where little elves make Christmas presents for good boys and girls. This toy workshop was a dangerous place. So dangerous, in fact, that Katie had to use her secret weapon. She pulled up her sleeve, revealing a mini computer in her right forearm. She installed a disk and closed her eyes. Instantly, a wealth of information loaded itself into her brain. Teddy watched in amazement.

"You're a Bio-ware?" Teddy asked her.

Katie nodded. "You're working with state of the art," she told him. "Our motto is 'more than human.'"

Teddy was impressed. Bio-wares were very special. They were part human, part machine. All they had to do was input any micro disk into their computer terminals. The next thing they knew, they were experts on medicine, weapons, science, anything! Teddy had a sudden flash of fear. If Katie thought this Toymaker guy was scary enough to force her to use her secret Bio-ware weapons, they could be heading for big trouble!

The Toymaker's workshop was in a dark, creepy part of town. As Teddy and Katie approached the entrance, the big Rex felt weak in the knees.

"Molly!" he cried out.

Katie whipped her head around. "Where?" she asked.

Teddy shook his head. "It's my dino-sense," he explained. "I felt Molly cry out for me. Something's happened to her." He started to walk back to the car. Katie raced off after him.

"You can't just waltz off for your girlfriend! We're on a case!" she shouted at Teddy. "This is just what they want. Summers put us together because he thinks we're a joke."

Teddy stopped in his tracks. "They *want* us to mess up?" he said slowly. Katie nodded. Now Teddy was mad. He marched right back up to the building. "It's time to take out the trash," he told Katie.

They found the Toymaker in a dark room filled with mounted butterflies. "Grid Police," Teddy introduced himself. "Coltrane and Teddy Rex."

"Last night one of your custom kill toys took out a Rex," Katie told the Toymaker.

The Toymaker didn't flinch. "What do you wish?" he asked.

Katie wanted two things—information about who ordered the dinocide, and a gun for Teddy.

When Teddy heard that, he jumped. Dinos didn't carry guns. They were nonviolent. But Katie wasn't letting him go out on the streets again without protection.

"Look, you're a dinosaur cop," she said. "An extinct species in an extinct profession. You want to stay alive? Then you need more than a ten-foot-long tail."

While Katie and Teddy were arguing, the Toymaker planted a toy beetle on the table. The beetle zipped toward Katie.

"Katie! Look out!" Teddy cried.

There was a huge explosion. When the dust cleared, Katie was dazed, but unharmed. The Toymaker was nowhere to be seen. "The little slug got away!" Katie shouted in frustration.

Teddy smiled and lifted his tail. There, wrapped in Teddy's tail, was the Toymaker. Sometimes that ten feet of tail came in handy.

"Let me down!" the Toymaker called out. Teddy moved over toward a hole in the wall and dangled the Toymaker over the street below. The Toymaker started to shake. Down was a very long way.

"Who did you sell your killer butterfly to?" Katie asked.

The Toymaker wasn't going to risk being dropped. "His name is Edge. He works for Kane," he spilled out. "Kane controls everything." Then the Toymaker said the most frightening thing of all. "Word on the street is that Kane kidnapped your little friend to make you stop the dino investigation!"

Katie was shocked. Kane had Sebastian! She quickly handcuffed the Toymaker to a pipe, called for back-up police to arrest him, and dragged Teddy to the car. They had to get over to Mr. Kane's New Eden compound right away!

CHAPTER THIRTEEN

The only way for Katie and Teddy to sneak into the New Eden compound was to enter with the Zapheads. Kane trusted the Zapheads. He'd created them, and Kane trusted only those things he had created. So Katie and Teddy made a little detour on their way to New Eden. They stopped at the Zapheads' hangout.

"Don't anybody stand up!" Katie shouted, her gun poised as she raced into the room. "We're here to trade your necks for weapons, a ride, and a meeting with your boss."

Spinner, one of the Zapheads, looked at Katie and laughed. "Yeah? Who's we?"

"Me," Katie answered.

"And me," Teddy added, stepping out of the darkness. With a whip of his tail, Teddy knocked out every one of the Zapheads but Spinner.

Spinner looked at the cop and the dino. Then he looked at his knocked-out pals. He had no choice but to drive Katie and Teddy into the compound. "You're crazy," Spinner told them. "Kane will make a Happy Meal out of us!"

But Katie wasn't worried. "They won't know what hit 'em!" she declared.

* * *

CRASH! The police garbage truck slammed through the clear glass wall of Mr. Kane's office in a storm of glass and truck parts. Teddy and Katie pulled themselves free from the wreckage and confronted the evil Mr. Kane.

"Where's Molly?" shouted Teddy.

"Where's Sebastian?" Katie demanded.

Mr. Kane looked at Katie and smirked. "He's in a cage where he belongs."

Katie didn't find that amusing. She pointed her gun at Kane. "Where's the cage?" she demanded.

"In my zoo."

Katie took off to find Sebastian, leaving Teddy to watch Mr. Kane.

"You let me down, Teddy," said Mr. Kane, with disapproval in his voice.

"Sorry to disappoint you. You're under arrest," Teddy responded.

But Mr. Kane didn't seem upset. In a matter of minutes his missiles were going to blow up the world. Billions of innocent people would be killed. But Mr. Kane didn't care. He was going to survive it, and that was all that mattered to him.

Kane walked over to the wall and pulled a lever. There sat a huge boat filled with animals. "It's my ark. I have brought pairs of all of the planet's insects, mammals, amphibians, birds, bacteria, et

cetera, here," he explained to Teddy. "The ingredients for a paradise."

Teddy looked around. There were no humans on the ark. No dinos either. Mr. Kane felt humans were a failed species. He had no need for them. But he did have two dinos in mind for his ark — Teddy and Molly.

"I'm pleased that you care for each other," Mr. Kane told Teddy. "You see, I need pairs of all animals."

And then Mr. Kane explained why he had plotted to have Oliver Rex murdered. "Oliver worked in Species Records and he became aware of my plan," Mr. Kane told Teddy. "Since he had access to my records, measures had to be taken."

"You killed him!" Teddy exclaimed.

Kane didn't respond. Instead, he called out to his associate, **Edge**. "Take care of him," he said, pointing to Teddy. Then he left the room.

Teddy was sure he was about to die. But he was wrong. Edge pressed a button on a remote control. The wall behind Teddy slid away. Quickly Teddy turned in the direction of the moving wall. That's when he spotted his beloved Molly. She was frozen in a tank, like one of Mr. Kane's Ice Fish. Now Teddy was really mad. The great Rex swept Edge up in his tail and sent him flying. Edge hit an overhead light and passed out in a shower of sparks.

Teddy knew it was only minutes before Mr. Kane would return. He had to melt Molly down—and quickly. Frantically he pushed at the buttons beside the tank. But Molly did not awaken from her frozen sleep.

Teddy was heartbroken. He pounded on the glass and let out a dino-sized howl of sorrow—one of the saddest sounds of the twenty-first century. Somehow, that was enough to awaken Molly. Her eyelids fluttered for a moment. Then her eyes opened. "Theo," she said quietly, touching her claw to the glass.

"Molly," Teddy answered as he opened the tank, and swept her into his arms.

CHAPTER FOURTEEN

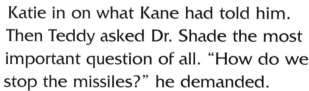

It had taken Katie a while to find Sebastian. But find him she did. He was just where Kane had said he would be—in a cage in the New Eden Zoo. The cage was guarded by Zapheads. That was actually a *good* thing, because the Zapheads were really stupid! It was easy for Katie to trick them into leaving the cage alone long enough for her to free Sebastian. Together, they ran off to find Teddy.

When they reached Mr. Kane's office, Katie couldn't believe her eyes. There was Molly Rex, seeming a bit chilly, but all right. And there was Teddy, looking every inch a police officer, interrogating a witness. Behind them was a giant ark, filled with pairs of animals.

Quickly, Teddy introduced Katie to the witness, Dr. Shade. Dr. Shade was Mr. Kane's personal doctor. She knew everything about Kane's dastardly plot to take over the world. Teddy quickly filled

Katie in on what Kane had told him. Then Teddy asked Dr. Shade the most important question of all. "How do we stop the missiles?" he demanded.

Dr. Shade smiled. She planned to go with Mr. Kane on the ark. "Only Kane can do that," she said. "He carries his remote control at all times."

There was something in the doctor's smile that really bugged Katie. She pushed Dr. Shade into the freezing tank. "Nighty-night," Katie said, slamming the door.

Boom! Boom! Boom! Suddenly three shots rang out from above. Mr. Kane was back—and armed! Katie pulled out her gun and shot back at him. Katie was a good shot—she caught Kane right in the arm. Kane got in a few good shots of his own, hitting Katie in the shoulder. She slumped over in pain. Teddy looked over at his wounded partner. Then he looked up at Kane. Teddy may have been created nonviolent, but his creator had forced him to become angrier than he had ever thought possible. Teddy grabbed Katie's gun and ran off after Mr. Kane.

Teddy looked down and followed the trail of Kane's blood. Kane couldn't have gone very far. But it was dark, and Teddy couldn't see very well.

Bang! A shot rang out in the darkness. Teddy was hit in the side. He fell to the ground in pain. Kane stood over him and laughed. "You must learn to accept defeat," the mad scientist said.

Teddy raised his gun. "You're . . . under . . . arrest," he said, struggling for air.

Mr. Kane could have run, but he didn't. He knew Teddy wouldn't kill him. "Violence is against your genetic code," he told the dino. "I know. I created you." But violence wasn't against Kane's genetic code. He jumped into a New Eden van and drove straight for Teddy!

Teddy wasn't going down without a fight. Quickly he wrapped his massive tail around a tree trunk. With all the strength he had left in him, Teddy used his tail to yank himself out of the way of the oncoming car.

As the car sped by, Teddy pulled out his gun and fired. Out shot a hook attached to a rope. The hook latched onto Kane's clothing, and Teddy reeled him in as if he had just caught a big fish! The remote control fell to the sidewalk. Teddy picked it up and pressed the stop-missile button, seconds before the planet was to be destroyed!

45

CHAPTER FIFTEEN

Days later, the New Eden compound had a whole new look. Children played on the lawns. Animals wandered about freely. Everyone was able to enjoy the things Mr. Kane had kept to himself for so long.

Katie and Teddy were on the front lawn, receiving an award. Not just for solving the two murders, but for saving the planet. Commissioner Lynch walked over to Teddy and saluted. He pinned a shiny silver badge on Teddy's lapel.

"Theodore Rex, it is my honor to promote you to Detective, First Class," he said, shaking hands with Teddy's claw. "You were right. We *can* rise above and make our dreams come true."

47

"Katie Coltrane," the commissioner continued, "I accept your resignation from Gun Command. But, for rising to the occasion, I transfer you to the Public Relations Department."

Teddy looked at her with surprise. "My old job?" he whispered.

"Yeah, I'm working my way down the ladder of success," she teased.

Then she smiled and shook the claw of the dinosaur who had once been her partner, but was now her friend.